In the Light of the Moon

of the Moon

& Other Bedtime Stories

For Sarah and Jennifer
and all their little ones
—S. M.

KINGFISHER
Larousse Kingfisher Chambers Inc.
80 Maiden Lane
New York, New York 10038
www.kingfisherpub.com

First published in 2001
10 9 8 7 6 5 4 3 2 1

LIBRARY OF CONGRESS CATALOGING-IN-PUBLICATION DATA
has been applied for.

ISBN 0-7534-5224-3

Printed in China
1TR/0701/SF/GRS(GRS)/157MA

In the Light of the Moon

& Other Bedtime Stories

Sam McBratney   Kady MacDonald Denton

KINGFISHER

NEW YORK

CONTENTS

———— ★ ————

FOREWORD

— ★ —

I GREW UP TO BE A storyteller, but I'm not sure why. When I was growing up, we used to play in the street. We played soccer and cricket and also games that people don't know nowadays, such as ship-shore-lifeboat and bar-the-door. I don't remember doing much reading at all.

On the other hand, my mother used to say to me, "Your nose was never out of a book," and I suppose she should know best. No doubt I discovered long ago that reading could take me on a journey to many other worlds, that I could be lots of different characters and share their wonderful, impossible adventures.

Is that why I grew up to tell stories? Perhaps I then discovered the fun of imagining my own worlds: at first for my own family to listen to, and after for other children to read in places near and far.

Wherever you are, here is a collection of characters and adventures for you to enjoy at bedtime, all wonderfully

illustrated by Kady MacDonald Denton.
The drawings are like little windows
into other worlds. Some of them made
me laugh out loud.

But why tell stories at *bedtime*? I've
often wondered about that too, because
after all, a good story is an anytime story.
Maybe it's simply that bedtime is best for the *people* involved, the tellers and
the listeners. No one is going anywhere, there is time—the telling of a story
and the hearing of it can happen without glances at the clock.

Reading to children, reading with them at the quiet end of the day, just
feels to me like one of the most natural and worthwhile things you can do.
And the benefits may last—who knows?—for all of a lifetime.

So I hope you enjoy this new collection of bedtime stories. Whether telling or
listening, may *your* nose spend a long and happy time *In the Light of the Moon*.

Sam McBratney

Ballymote 2001

STOP DAYDREAMING, SPEEDWELL BUNTING

★

ONCE UPON A TIME and far away there was a Tooth Fairy who loved to daydream. His name was Speedwell Bunting, but his friends called him Bunty for short.

Now Bunty never did a lick of work, not if he could help it.

He lay around in the sun, eating fresh fruit and honeycakes,

daydreaming about being a great hero who saved his friends from danger in the nick of time.

Above all he dreamed of going on a tooth hunt and bringing back a wonderful tooth.

That was his favorite daydream, for tooth hunting is the most dangerous thing a Tooth Fairy can do. There are storms of wind and snow. There are birds with snipper-snapper beaks, spiders with clinging webs, and dazzling lights in the night sky. Worst of all is the fear of being seen by a human—for if a child sees a Tooth Fairy, then that fairy disappears forever.

No. Tooth hunting was so dangerous that Bunty never did it. He only daydreamed.

One morning, while Bunty was riding his pet frog, an amazing thing happened. He *found* a tooth. It was just lying there at the bottom of a dried-up pond. "Someone must have dropped it on the way back from a tooth hunt," thought Bunty.

Now, Tooth Fairies use teeth for many things, because teeth are so tough. A good tooth is worth its weight in gold, and this one was as perfect a tooth as could be.

Bunty was so pleased that he couldn't wait to show it to his friend Skye.

"You should try to find out who owns it, Bunty," said Skye.

"Who owns it? *I* own it—it's mine now! I'm off to the market, where I'm going to sell it for gold!"

Sure enough, Bunty set off for the market to sell the wonderful tooth. On the way he stopped on the bridge over the river and began to daydream as usual.

"How much will I get?" he wondered. "A whole pocketful of gold? Enough to buy ten hives of honeybees?

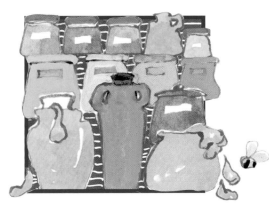

And if ten hives of honeybees make ten pots of honey each, that makes a hundred pots to sell!

I'll have the money to buy the things I've always wanted—like a new waistcoat. I could easily end up the best-dressed Tooth Fairy in the country.

I might even marry the Fairy Princess —and if I do *that*, what's to stop me from becoming King one day?"

Oh, what a thought: to be King of the Tooth Fairies! That was even better than lying in the sun, eating fresh fruit and honeycakes. Bunty spun right around with joy . . . and knocked the tooth off the bridge.

Down it went—down, down, down. He watched it fall into the river far below. What a sight that was, to see the lovely tooth disappear forever. Bunty felt like crying—but he didn't.

"Just forget about it, Bunty," Skye said when she heard the sad story.

"I can't forget," groaned the miserable Bunty.

"Well it wasn't really yours in the first place," said Skye. "Get yourself another one."

"How?"

"You could go on a tooth hunt."

"Are you *crazy*?" cried Bunty.

"I'm not crazy. Stop daydreaming, Speedwell Bunting, and go get a tooth of your own."

For the next few days Bunty tried to pretend that he hadn't lost the tooth in the river—that he'd zoomed down and caught it in the nick of time. That didn't work, though. Daydreaming wasn't any good now; he'd held the real thing in his own two hands.

Then he began to think. "Others go tooth hunting, so why not me? I can probably be as brave as anyone else if I try; and besides, Skye thinks I can do it. I *will* go on a tooth hunt. I'll go tomorrow!"

And he did. Off he flew with a coin strapped to his back, for as everyone knows, teeth are not free. The Tooth Fairies have to pay for them.

He flew through the storms of wind and snow.

He dodged the birds with the snipper-snapper beaks.

He fought off the spiders with their clinging webs.

He flew into the dazzling lights of the far city.

Taking care not to be seen by a human, he squeezed through a keyhole and flew up the stairs to where a perfect tooth—a top front tooth!—had been left under a pillow.

In a hurry now, Bunty put down his coin. It would be discovered when the morning came. Then he picked up the tooth and sped away as softly as a whisper with wings.

In this way and at last, Speedwell Bunting came home with as fine a tooth as you could wish to see. Many of his friends were there to meet him and say how brave he was, including Skye.

"Good job, Bunty," she said to him.

Nowadays Bunty keeps hives of honeybees, and he has a fancy waistcoat for every day of the week. He's much too busy to lie around in the sunshine, and he doesn't dream about marrying a princess, because Skye is his wife now. But when the work is done and all is quiet, he still likes to close his eyes and imagine many things that might—or might not—be. . . .

BROTHER BEAR

★

THERE WAS ONCE a farmer bear who owned some fields in a high valley. Although his land was rocky land and not so good for growing things, the farmer bear worked hard and managed to produce root vegetables and sometimes even corn.

One year there happened to be a good, long summer of sunshine and warm rain. When all was harvested, the farmer bear found that he had three full sacks of food for the winter. But he didn't need three sacks of food—two were more than enough for him, so he wondered what to do with the third one.

As he was thinking about the problem he remembered something his mother used to say to him many years ago: "You should always, always share what you have. If you share with others, you'll be much happier than if you keep everything for yourself."

When the bear remembered these words, he thought of his brother who lived across the valley. And this is what he said to himself: "I have three sacks of food. Two sacks will get me through the winter; I won't eat any more than that. I will give the third one to my brother in case he doesn't have enough."

That night the bear set out for his brother's house with a sack of food on his back. He walked down his side of the valley, over the bridge that crossed the stream, and up the hill, where he left the sack of food in his brother's barn. He did all this at night, because he knew his brother well—his brother would want to pay him for the food, and the bear didn't want to be paid. It was a gift.

In the morning, however, the bear noticed something strange. He still had three sacks of food in his shed.

"How can this be?" he thought. "I gave one away last night. Did I have *four* sacks of food instead of three? Oh well, it means that I can afford to give my brother another sack."

That night the bear walked down his side of the valley, over the bridge that crossed the stream, and up the hill, where he left another sack of food in his brother's barn.

And when the morning came, he found that he still had the same number of sacks as before. Three of them.

It was the most peculiar thing that the bear had ever come across. Was this some kind of magic, he wondered? No matter what he did, he still ended up with three sacks of food!

"Never mind," the bear said to himself, "magic or not, food is food, and it can always be eaten. I will bring my brother one more sack."

That night, when he set out for his brother's house, there was a full moon shining above the valley. Even though it was nighttime, the bear was able to watch his bent-over shadow bobbing along in front of him.

As he reached the bridge he saw someone coming toward him in the pale light, and this someone also had a sack upon his back. Before long they met face-to-face as they crossed the bridge.

The other someone shouted out, amazed, "A—ha! So it was *you*, my brother!"

The bear shouted out in delight, "Now I see! It was *you*, my brother, and not magic!"

Each brother had been trying to help out the other one. They hugged each other, they laughed at the idea of magic sacks of food, and they talked about old times under the moon.

BENTLEY—
GO GENTLY

★

IN DAYS GONE BY there lived
a country gentleman and his pig.
The gentleman's name was Arthur, and
his pig was named Bentley. To most people
Bentley didn't look like much; but then, most people
don't know a lot about pigs. They wouldn't know that Bentley
had once won first prize at an agricultural show.

One important morning Arthur planted an apple tree in his garden. "There we are!" he said to Bentley when the job was done. "Let us hope that this tree provides us with lots of apples for many years to come."

Then he went inside to change his clothes, for he was expecting a lady visitor that afternoon, and he wanted to look his best.

Even Bentley got a jolly good scrub.

"And Bentley, don't go rolling in the mud," said Arthur. "Remember, this is a special day, a day for going *gently*."

The lady visitor, looking very smart, arrived in her open-top car. She had brought along her little dog Poppy, who knew how to shake-a-hand.

"Go on, Poppy, shake-a-hand," said the lady. Sure enough, Poppy gave Arthur one of her paws.

"Jolly well done!" declared Arthur, with scarcely a glance in Bentley's direction. No one could doubt that Poppy was the star of the show.

Poppy also knew how to sit-up-and-beg for one of the treats that the lady visitor carried in her purse. Bentley tried to sit-up-and-beg too, but it wasn't easy. He toppled over backward with a mighty thud.

"Oops!" cried Arthur. "Remember, Bentley—go *gently*."

It was very disappointing. Bentley loved a treat and he didn't get one.

"Never mind," said the lady visitor. "You're just a pig, after all—and pigs aren't as clever as dogs when it comes to doing tricks. Let's all go out for a walk!"

So they all went for a walk. Now, Bentley liked to wander where the ditches were deep and the mud came over your knees—but not today. . . .

Today was a day for going gently. Arthur wasn't even wearing his galoshes! With impeccable manners he held the lady's hand to help her through a gate.

On the way home the lady visitor threw a stick for Poppy to chase, which she did. She chased it very well. And when she brought the stick back, her reward was a great big hug.

"Ooh, my *clever* Popsy-wopsy!" said her mistress, producing a whopper of a treat from a pretty pouch in her purse.

There were lovely treats: some black, some orange, some long and thin, and a few short, fat ones. Bentley really longed for a treat too, but he didn't get one. Or a hug.

"Never mind," the lady said to him. "You're just a pig, after all— we don't expect you to fetch sticks like my Popsy-wopsy!"

They went back into the house for a cup of tea. After some quiet conversation the lady visitor looked up and said, "I wonder where your silly pig has gone, Arthur? He probably wishes he were a dog, you know."

Arthur smiled and moved a little closer to her on the sofa. "I wonder . . . would you like another buttered scone, Victoria?"

No one ever found out the answer to that question—that was the very moment when the door crashed open and Bentley ran into the room with a stick in his mouth.

That was some stick! One end had a few twiggy branches, and the other end looked like a ball of wet mud. The sight of it sent poor little Poppy running for her life! As Arthur opened his mouth to shout something —probably "Bentley, go gently!"—he saw that he was too late. His pig had dumped the enormous stick in the lady visitor's lap!

And Bentley seemed very pleased—as if *this* should be worth a treat or two.

"Ooh-ooh-ooh!" squealed the lady visitor. "Get it off of me!"

"That's my new apple tree!" cried Arthur.

"This is my best dress!"

"I only planted it this morning!"

"Good heavens, Arthur, the brute has brought me a whole tree—a filthy *tree*!"

Such a hullabaloo! There was so much going on that no one noticed as Bentley finished off the bag of treats and then the buttered scones.

The lady visitor left soon after with Poppy cradled safely in her arms. "I'm glad you're not a *pig*," she whispered in her doggy's little ear.

At the door of the car Arthur said good-bye. "You must come again, Victoria," he added hopefully.

The car zoomed away. Little Poppy looked back with big, wide-open eyes, still amazed by all she had seen that day.

When they had gone, Arthur said some fierce words to Bentley about how to behave in public. Then he planted the apple tree once more.

"And this time," he said to his venerable pig, "leave it ALONE."

Bentley went for a rollicking roll in the mud. He couldn't shake-a-hand or sit-up-and-beg or curl up small on a lady's knee. But he looked more than happy to be a gentleman's pig.

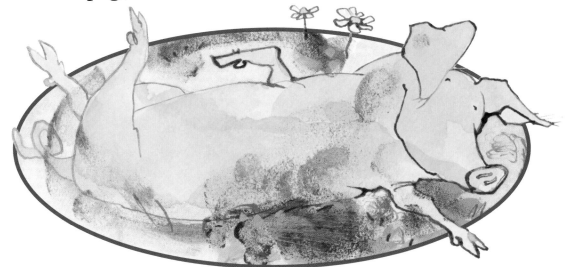

IN THE LIGHT OF THE MOON

★

NOT SO FAR AWAY from here—and not so long ago, either—there lived a wise old mouse and his three young mice.

The first young mouse was named Cob, and he was the most grown-up; the second young mouse was named Hazel, and she was the middle one; and the youngest of the mice was little Berry-Berry. They all lived together in the warm, dry cellar of an old, old house.

One day the old mouse
took his young mice to visit
their cousins in the cornfield.
They had a wonderful day
playing in the sunshine
and the rain.

They ran in and out
of the puddles . . .

danced on their
shadows in the sun . . .

and swayed back and
forth on the ears of
yellow corn, which is a
thing mice love to do.

But at last the old mouse said it was time to go home.

"The sun is going down," he said, "and I never like to be out in the light of the moon."

The young mice did not know what he meant, for they had never seen the moon.

"What is it like?" asked Cob.

"Is it big and scary?" asked Hazel.

"Is the moon as big as me?" laughed little Berry-Berry.

"Oh, it's big," the old mouse said, and they set off for home.

They left the cornfield through a hole in the hedge and followed the hedge as far as the oak tree that grew beside the stream. Here the old mouse looked up as though there might be something in the sky.

"Are you watching for the moon?" asked Cob.

"How will we know it if we see it?" asked Hazel.

"I think the moon lives up a tree!" cried little Berry-Berry.

It was time to cross the stream. Crossing the stream took longer than usual, for the water was flowing quickly after heavy rain. On the far bank the old mouse paused, and he looked up as if there might be something in the sky.

"It's almost dark," whispered Cob.

"The dark is fine," said the old mouse. "It is better than the light of the moon. Stay together and we won't get lost."

"I'll hold on to your tail," said Cob.

"I'll hold on to Cob's tail," said Hazel.

"I'll hold on to my own tail so it won't get lost!" cried little Berry-Berry.

The old mouse and his young mice walked along a ditch as far as the garden gate, where they stopped once more. The young mice had never been out when the world was so still.

"It's very quiet," said Hazel.

"The quiet is fine," the old mouse told them softly, looking up at the sky. "We'll be quiet too. We're almost home."

The old mouse was in a hurry as he crept under the garden gate, with his young mice following behind.

Then Hazel noticed that all of a sudden they had shadows! The seed heads of some dandelions began to glow as a light in the night sky lit up the garden path.

"It's the moon!" cried Cob.

"I see the beautiful moon,"
said Hazel.

"And the moon sees *me*!" sang out
little Berry-Berry.

The three of them gazed up,
eyes shining in the light. . . .

But then something else was in the sky, and it wasn't the moon: this something else was big and getting bigger—a great, dark swooping shadow with a beak and wings and claws and eyes. Dropping from the sky it came. . . . "Be quick!" the old mouse cried. "It wants its dinner!"

Across the cracks between
the stones, in and out of the
broken pots and down
the spout and through
the hole behind the spout
ran the young mice;
and they ran as if the
something-in-the-sky were as
close behind them as their tails!

None of them stopped
running until they were
inside the cellar and
safe at last, their little
hearts beating like
drums.

That night the old mouse asked his young mice what they remembered about their day in the cornfield.

"Jumping shadows was good," said Cob.

"Not as good as running in the puddles," said Hazel.

"Swinging on the corn was best of all!" laughed little Berry-Berry.

The old mouse tucked them in gently. "There is something else I want you to remember," he said, "something that wanted its dinner."

The young mice looked up at the wise old mouse and nodded their little heads, for they had learned a lot that day. None of them would forget the something-in-the-sky that they had seen in the light of the moon.

THE FOX
WHO LIKED EGGS

★

ONCE UPON A TIME there was a young fox who happened to be fond of eggs. As a matter of fact, they were her favorite food, although she hardly ever got any. Eggs were scarce in the forest. Now, there was a farmyard near the forest where the young fox had her den, and in this farmyard lived four most intelligent birds: Henny Penny, Goosey Loosey, Turkey Lurkey, and Ducky Lucky.

Where there are birds, there are eggs; so one fine day the fox trotted down to the farmyard to see what she could see.

The hen was up a tree.

The goose was sitting on a rain barrel.

The duck was paddling in a puddle.

And the turkey was perched on a pile of logs.

The four of them looked half-asleep!

"Good morning," said the fox. "May I ask why you are all so quiet today?"

"Because we are thinking," came the reply.

The fox was thinking too. She was thinking how lovely it would be if she could run away with one of the eggs she'd just spotted—but she put the thought out of her head. That tough old turkey would jump on her, and the others would peck her black and blue.

"What are you thinking *about*?" she asked pleasantly.

"I was just wondering how high is the sky," said Henny Penny.

"I was just wondering how far does the wind blow," said Goosey Loosey.

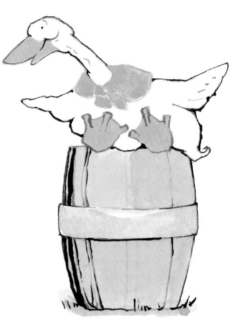

"I was just wondering how dark is the darkest night," said Turkey Lurkey.

"And I was wondering how deep is the deepest puddle," said Ducky Lucky. "You wouldn't happen to know that, would you?"

The eyes of the young fox seemed to glitter as she did some thinking of her own. Then she carefully shook her head. "Oh, I wouldn't know," she said. "I'm only a fox, you see. The one you want to speak to is the Wise Old Bird of the Forest, who lives in the sycamore tree. They say he knows . . . everything."

"Really?" quacked Ducky Lucky.

"Oh yes," said the fox, "he answers questions every morning at ten o'clock sharp, and that's not the most amazing thing. The most amazing thing is that he only charges one fresh egg for each question, no matter how hard it is!" Then the fox smiled at the four most intelligent birds and went on her way.

Now, Henny Penny, Goosey Loosey, Turkey Lurkey, and Ducky Lucky did not often go into the woods, but they couldn't help thinking how nice it would be to have their intelligent questions answered for a change. So they set off early the next morning to see the Wise Old Bird who knew . . . everything.

Marching two-by-two along the shady forest path, Henny Penny, Goosey Loosey, Turkey Lurkey, and Ducky Lucky came upon the sycamore tree in the woods. Sure enough, standing up high in the fork of the tree was the Wise Old Bird.

"We have some questions for you, if you don't mind," Henny Penny called out.

"Pay me an egg and ask what you like," said a voice in reply.

As Henny Penny placed her egg by the trunk of the tree, she said, "I would very much like to know. . . . How high is the sky?"

"Very high," said the Wise Old Bird. "Next please."

 Goosey Loosey stepped forward with her egg. "I wonder, could you tell me. . . . How far does the wind blow?"

 "Very far," said the Wise Old Bird. "Next please."

 It was Turkey Lurkey's turn. "My question is. . . . How dark is the darkest night?"

 "Very very dark," said the Wise Old Bird. "Next!"

 Ducky Lucky stepped forward with her egg. "I would like to know. . . . How deep is the deepest puddle?"

 "As deep as could be," said the Wise Old Bird. "Good-bye."

That was all. The four most intelligent birds journeyed home quickly now that they had no eggs to carry—but they weren't really happy. They weren't happy because they didn't think that they had been given good answers by the Wise Old Bird.

"I *know* the sky is *very* high," grumbled Henny Penny. "I don't think he's any wiser than I am."

"I've always known that the darkest night is *very* dark," said Turkey Lurkey. "I don't think he's wiser than any of us."

"I don't think he's wise at *all*," said Goosey Loosey.

"If you ask me, he's really very silly!" quacked Ducky Lucky.

Back in the forest the Wise Old Bird was slowly climbing down from the sycamore tree. As he came down he paused now and then to pluck a feather from his coat. The feathers came off easily, for he wasn't a bird at all. He wasn't old, either, and as a matter of fact he wasn't a he.

She was a fox who happened to be very fond of eggs.

THE STORY OF PETITE COCCINELLE

★

SOMEWHERE across the sea in a corner of an Irish garden there is the greenhouse where Mr. Thomas grows his tomatoes.

Every year people say to him: "Mr. Thomas, how do you grow such juicy big tomatoes? You must have a wonderful secret!"

Then Mr. Thomas smiles and thinks to himself, "My ladybugs."

This is the story of one of Mr. Thomas's ladybugs. He was called Petite Coccinelle because he was a French ladybug.

"*Petite Coccinelle, Petite Coccinelle, tu veux jouer à cache-cache?*"

Every spring morning, those words began the day for Petite Coccinelle. They were French words because he lived in France. His friends were calling him out to play. He lived in one of the lovely lime trees that grow along the streets of Paris. The people passing by on the sidewalk below hardly ever looked up;

and so they hardly ever saw Petite Coccinelle playing with his friends among the leaves.

Sometimes he flew to the flowers in the window boxes to see if the aphids tasted any better there. And on warm afternoons Petite Coccinelle liked to visit the park where children played in the shade and where visitors to Paris found a cool spot for their picnics.

Now, one very hot day he landed on a piece of lettuce just as someone popped it into a lunchbox! The lid closed, and for Petite Coccinelle the world grew darker than it had ever been.

The next morning his friends called for him as usual. They said: *"Petite Coccinelle, Petite Coccinelle, tu veux jouer à cache-cache?"* When they heard no answer, they thought that perhaps he had gone to live in another lime tree and that he would come back to visit them soon.

But Petite Coccinelle was inside a lunchbox, in a car, on a ferry, on the way to another country. The people who owned the lunchbox were Irish, and they were going back to Ireland.

That was a long and jiggly journey for a ladybug. Many hours went by before someone took the lid off the box—and then how wonderful it was to see the light once more! Up and away flew Petite Coccinelle as fast as he could fly, for he wanted to find his friends again and hear them call: *"Petite Coccinelle, Petite Coccinelle, tu veux jouer à cache-cache?"*

But this was not France. It was Ireland, and the lime trees of Paris were far away.

"Hey!" said an angry white butterfly. "What are you doing in my cabbage patch?"

Petite Coccinelle flew away to some tall flowers, but a cross black beetle shouted out, "You there! What are you doing on my foxgloves?"

This time Petite Coccinelle landed on a fir tree.

"Little ladybug," said a spider softly, "why don't you come over here and play with me?"

Although Petite Coccinelle didn't understand a word they said, he knew not to trust spiders, and he knew that the butterfly and the beetle didn't want to be his friends. He flew off to hide among some roses, feeling tired and lonely and lost.

Petite Coccinelle spent the night curled up inside a rosebud. In the morning, forgetting where he was, he expected to hear his friends say: *"Petite Coccinelle, Petite Coccinelle, tu veux jouer à cache-cache?"* Instead, he heard only the wind begin to blow.

The wind began to blow and the bush began to shake. The wind blew Petite Coccinelle across the fields as easily as it blows the seed head of a dandelion—until at last he fell to the ground, exhausted, on a patch of grass. A drop of rain as big as himself splashed on his back, almost turning him right over.

"How can I live without my lime tree—" thought Petite Coccinelle, who was wet all through and feeling cold, "how can I live without my friends?"

Later that day Mr. Thomas stepped into his garden to look for ladybugs. He needed some of the little insects badly, because aphids were sucking the juice out of his tomato plants. Some gardeners kill aphids with poisonous sprays, but Mr. Thomas didn't like to use poison on food that people eat. He liked to use ladybugs, because ladybugs gobble up aphids all day long.

Eventually he found one half hidden among the stones of the path, but it didn't look very lively when he picked it up.

"Well now, little fellow—you look as if you've had a hard time," said Mr. Thomas, carrying him to the greenhouse. Here he set Petite Coccinelle on a leaf and closed the door behind him.

It was warm and bright in the greenhouse. Once he was feeling dry and had eaten well, Petite Coccinelle noticed that there were other ladybugs in this interesting place.

At first Petite Coccinelle was too shy to join in their games, and he couldn't understand what they said because the words they used were English words. But he watched and listened, and he could see that they would like to be his friends. As the days went by he didn't feel so lonely, and he didn't think so often about the lime trees of Paris.

Later that summer one of the ladybugs called out to him: "*Little Ladybug, Little Ladybug, are you there— are you coming out to play?*" And he did go out.

He went out to play hide-and-seek the way he used to do, but with new friends; this time across the sea in the quiet of an Irish garden.

BIG BOG FROG
AND LITTLE UMBEL

★

THERE ARE PARTS of the world where the days are warm and the nights are never cold. In one such place there lived a frog, and his home was a quiet pond beneath the shady trees.

Now Big Bog Frog was a mighty frog. No other frog

could hop as high as Big Bog Frog could hop. And no other frog could croak as loudly as Big Bog Frog could croak. He had large bulging eyes, and his shining skin was a speckled green. Big Bog Frog was a mighty frog, but he was also as mean as he could be.

He chased away the other frogs who came near his pond.

He chased away the birds who swooped to drink,

and he tried to eat the dainty dragonflies who flew down to lay their eggs.

"This is *my* pond," croaked Big Bog Frog. "I am . . . THE BOSS."

One day a baby elephant wandered near the pond beneath the trees. Little Umbel was round and plump and gray with small, bright eyes in her wrinkled face.

Although she was tiny for an elephant, Little Umbel was the most enormous thing that Big Bog Frog had ever seen, and he could hardly wait to make fun of her.

"Hey, Big Ears—where'd you get that nose?" laughed Big Bog Frog. "Hey, Big Nose—where'd you get those *ears*?" He was good at name calling because he did it so often.

Little Umbel, who liked her ears and liked her nose, didn't say anything to Big Bog Frog. She ambled away, as elephants do, looking for juicy plants to chew.

The next morning, as Big Bog Frog relaxed on a lily pad, Little Umbel wandered by once more. She ambled along, as elephants do, with her dangly-down trunk almost trailing on the ground.

"Hey, Big Ears!" shouted Big Bog Frog. "Watch your *toes* don't trip on your *nose*." Then he laughed so much that he almost slid off the lily pad into the water.

Little Umbel didn't say anything to Big Bog Frog. She dipped her trunk into the pond and began to drink. As Little Umbel began to drink, Big Bog Frog began to sink.

Drink—drink—drink . . .

Sink . . .   sink . . .   sink.

The more Little Umbel sucked and drank, the more the lily pad sank and sank—until Big Bog Frog found himself sitting on the squelchy mud at the bottom. His water had been drunk down to the very . . . last . . . drop.

"My pond!" croaked Big Bog Frog. "It's gone!"

No one has ever seen a frog as hopping mad as Big Bog Frog in the mud. He hopped his highest hops and he croaked his loudest croaks. But Little Umbel ambled away—as elephants do—looking for juicy plants to chew.

BARGAIN
BEAR

★

SOME TEDDY BEARS are young, and some are not so young; but only a very few are as old as the bear in this story.

Fifty years ago, or maybe sixty years ago, a little girl named Mary Rose bought a teddy bear with the coins she had saved in her piggy bank.

Mary Rose loved the look in her teddy's big, brown eyes and the feel of his soft fur.

She called her new bear "Growly Bear" because he growled when she tipped him up.

Her mommy sewed a G on the bottom of one foot and a B on the bottom of the other.

He became a very special friend and went everywhere with Mary Rose.

Then one sad day Mary Rose lost Growly Bear on a train. She tried to find him again—but Growly Bear ended up in the Lost and Found, hidden behind all the umbrellas, hats, and gloves.

"Someone is sure to come for me soon," Growly Bear may have said to himself, trying to look on the bright side. But no one did.

No one came for him until that windy day in the fall when everything in the Lost and Found was put up for sale, and Growly Bear was bought by a boy named Ronnie and his mom. They thought that he was very cheap—a bargain bear, in fact. And that's what they called him: Bargain Bear.

There wasn't much room in Ronnie's house for toys, so his new Bargain Bear got squashed and a little bit bashed.

Bargain Bears are tough, though, and they don't mind squashing and bashing. Besides, Ronnie loved reading, and he read many a story to his good friend Bargain Bear.

After some years had gone by, Ronnie's mom had to make room for different things—Ronnie was almost grown-up now and needed room for his record player and his books— so she sold Bargain Bear to the secondhand store.

"Someone is sure to come for me," Bargain Bear may have thought to cheer himself up, but it isn't easy to look on the bright side when you're not the brand new bear you used to be. And by now he had lost his lovely deep growl; he no longer made a noise when you tipped him up.

How long was he there in the secondhand store? It might have been years, for Bargain Bears are not good at knowing the time. Then one day he was spotted by twin brothers— and they bought him!

Living with brothers who love soccer can be rough. Bob and Stephen used Bargain Bear as a goalie. One unlucky day, while kicking their ball in the house, they broke one of their mother's flying ducks and had the ball taken away from them. So then they used Bargain Bear as the ball!

Before long those twins broke another duck. Their mom marched them straight to bed and gave Bargain Bear to a man who came collecting things for charity.

Sitting in the charity store, Bargain Bear may have worried that no one would want him. How can you look on the bright side when you've lost your growl and you've got a loose eye and there are holes in your body where the stuffing shows through? But then. . . .

Then a girl called Veronica saw him and loved him at once! She brought him home that same day because he was very, *very* cheap—cheap enough to buy with her allowance.

Veronica gave Bargain Bear a bath and put bandages on him when he was dry. Then she set him up high where he could not be chewed or thrown around, because Veronica had small brothers and sisters who often broke her toys.

When nighttime came, Veronica would bring her Bargain Bear down for a snuggle. One morning her brothers found him under the covers of her bed. They had a tug-of-war with Bargain Bear—they pulled and pulled until one of his arms came off!

Everybody was very upset. Mother bought Veronica a brand new panda, which *did* help; but what could they do with Bargain Bear?

"Mommy, don't just throw him away!" cried Veronica.

"No of course I won't throw him away, I'll give him to the toy hospital," said her mother.

And she did. She gave him away to the man who fixed toys.

How long did Bargain Bear sit in the back of the toy mender's workshop? No one knows. He may have wished for a boy or a girl to take him home, but a bear with a torn *arm* . . .? Even someone who tried to look on the bright side couldn't have been too hopeful that such a thing would happen.

At last, however, the toy mender got busy with needle, thread, and buttons. He sewed the arm back on; did a patch here; put a patch there—until he looked at Bargain Bear and said, "As good as new!"

That was a bit of an exaggeration, but Bargain Bear certainly looked much improved. He even had a new growly voice, which must have pleased him a lot. When you tipped him up, his growl was as grand as it had ever been.

"*Now* you're worth a pretty penny," the toy mender said to him.

He sold Bargain Bear to an antique store, a store full of old and very expensive things. Bargain Bear may have wondered who would buy him, for this was not the sort of store that children came into. They didn't want old irons or old furniture or faded old plates.

But then came the week before Christmas. The street outside sparkled under a host of many-colored lights,

and the shoppers hurrying by hardly seemed to notice the flakes of snow falling from a black sky. A lady and her husband pushed open the door of the antique store. They had come to buy a clock for a friend.

The lady glanced up at the teddy bear in the window; then looked again. The second time she noticed a G on his right foot.

"Oh my goodness!" she said. "It couldn't be. . . . Could it?"

"Look at the other foot, Mary Rose," said her husband, who had often heard the story of Growly Bear and how he had the letter G on one foot and B on the other.

"It's there—the B!" cried Mary Rose. "It's *him*, my Growly Bear! After all these years he's mine again—I wonder where he's been? Isn't this something?"

It really was. Mary Rose paid one hundred dollars and took her Growly Bear home. "This time I'm not going to lose you," she told him.

And she didn't. He still lives with Mary Rose, and I should think he's pleased, don't you? After all, it's not so hard to look on the bright side when someone loves you as much as that.